American Assoc. for the Advancement of Science

Daily Programme of the Seventeenth Meeting

of the American Association for the Advancement of Science commencing

Wednesday, August 5, 1868, in the City of Chicago, Illinois

American Assoc. for the Advancement of Science

Daily Programme of the Seventeenth Meeting
of the American Association for the Advancement of Science commencing Wednesday, August 5, 1868, in the City of Chicago, Illinois

ISBN/EAN: 9783337406202

Printed in Europe, USA, Canada, Australia, Japan

Cover: Foto ©Andreas Hilbeck / pixelio.de

More available books at **www.hansebooks.com**

DAILY PROGRAMME

OF THE

SEVENTEENTH MEETING

OF THE

AMERICAN ASSOCIATION

FOR THE

ADVANCEMENT OF SCIENCE,

COMMENCING WEDNESDAY, AUGUST 5, 1868,

IN THE

CITY OF CHICAGO, ILLINOIS.

CHICAGO:
Church, Goodman and Donnelley, Printers to the Academy of Sciences
1868.

Officers of the Chicago Meeting.

Dr. B. A. GOULD,	*President*
Col. CHARLES WHITTLESEY,	*Vice-President.*
Prof. JOSEPH LOVERING,	*Permanent Secretary.*
Prof. A. P. ROCKWELL,	*General Secretary.*
Dr. A. L. ELWYN,	*Treasurer.*

STANDING COMMITTEE.

Dr. B. A. GOULD.
Col. CHARLES WHITTLESEY.
Prof. JOSEPH LOVERING.
Prof. A. P. ROCKWELL.

Prof. J. S. NEWBERRY.
Prof. WOLCOTT GIBBS.
Prof. C. S. LYMAN.
Dr A. L. ELWYN.

LOCAL COMMITTEE.

Hon. J. YOUNG SCAMMON, *Chairman.*
Dr. WILLIAM STIMPSON, *Secretary.*

Prof. EDMUND ANDREWS.
Col. J. F. BEATY.
Prof. J. V. Z. BLANEY.
E. W. BLATCHFORD, Esq.
Lt.-Gov. WM. BROSS.
E. S. CHESBROUGH, Esq.
Col. EDWARD DANIELS.
WM. E. DOGGETT, Esq.
Col. J. W. FOSTER.
DAVID A. GAGE, Esq.
Dr. WALTER HAY.

Hon. E. B. McCAGG.
Dr. JOHN H. RAUCH.
CHARLES H. REED, Esq.
Hon. J. B. RICE.
Prof. T. H. SAFFORD.
E. H. SHELDON, Esq.
PERRY H. SMITH, Esq.
DANIEL THOMPSON, Esq.
GEORGE C. WALKER, Esq.
Hon. C. L. WILSON.
Dr. JOHN M. WOODWORTH.

LOCAL SUB-COMMITTEES.

On Reception — Messrs. RAUCH, SAFFORD, McCAGG, RICE and BROSS.

On Lodging and Entertainment — Messrs. SCAMMON, McCAGG, DOGGETT, BROSS, THOMPSON, GAGE and HAY.

On Rooms — Messrs. BLANEY, WALKER and ANDREWS.

On Finance — Messrs. DOGGETT, WALKER, BEATY and BROSS.

On Excursions — Messrs. DANIELS, SHELDON, BEATY, BLATCHFORD, WILSON and SMITH.

On Invitation, Correspondence and Printing — Messrs. HAY, WOODWORTH and STIMPSON.

On Railroads — Messrs. CHESBROUGH, FOSTER, SHELDON and BLANEY.

RULES OF MEMBERSHIP.

"RULE 1. Members of scientific societies or learned bodies having in view any of the objects of this Association, and publishing transactions, shall be considered [permanent] members on subscribing to these rules.

"RULE 2. Collegiate professors, also civil engineers and architects, who have been employed in the construction or superintendence of public works, may become [permanent] members on subscribing to these rules.

"RULE 3. Persons not embraced in the above provisions may become members of the Association upon recommendation in writing by two members, nomination by the Standing Committee, and election by a majority of the members present.

"*Resolution* 9. Associate members may be admitted for one, two, or three years, as they shall choose at the time of admission — to be elected in the same way as permanent members, and to pay the same dues. They shall have all the social and scientific privileges of members, without taking part in the business."

The admission fee of new members is five dollars, in addition to the annual subscription, which, including the price of the volume of Proceedings, is three dollars for all members. These dues should be paid at as early a period as possible. They will be received by the Permanent Secretary, at the office of the Local Committee. According to Rule 21 of the Constitution, no person shall be considered a member until the dues for the meeting are paid.

The general sessions will be held in Library Hall, which has been generously placed at the disposal of the Local Committee by the Young Men's Library Association. This hall is situated in Metropolitan Block, corner of LaSalle and Randolph streets. The sections will meet in two smaller halls in the same building. The sections of Mathematics, Physics and Chemistry will meet in Caledonian Hall, and the section of Natural History in the hall formerly occupied by the Academy of Sciences.

The public generally are invited to attend the meetings, both general and sectional. Foreign scientific gentlemen, who may be in the city, are particularly invited to attend, and to make themselves known to the Local Committee.

The Local Committee will be in attendance at their room in the Sherman House, adjoining the room of the Permanent Secretary — the members of the committee being distinguished by a badge, in order that they may be easily found by those desiring information. Each member of the committee will be provided with a list of hotels, with the reduced rates at which some of them offer accommodations.

Members, and those who wish to become members, are requested, on their arrival in Chicago, to proceed, as soon as convenient, to the office of the Local Committee, to register their names, professions, residences, the routes of travel by which they have reached the city, and (as soon as may be) their place of abode. At this office they will be furnished with their "members' tickets" and other documents, and with a map of the city.

Letters directed to the care of the Association, may be found at the office of Mr. Robson, Librarian of the Y. M. Association, on the same floor with Library Hall.

The Daily Programme will be ready for distribution in Library Hall, at the convening of the general session, each day at 10, A.M. Or, it may be subsequently found at the Librarian's office.

The Reading Room of the Young Men's Association, containing the chief daily papers and other periodical literature of the country will be open to the members during the week of the meeting.

The following Institutions and places of interest will be open to the visits of the members of the Association during their stay in the city. They may be visited by the Association in a body, or by the members singly. In the latter case, the member's ticket will secure admittance when any such ticket is required.

THE UNIVERSITY OF CHICAGO.

This Institution is situated on Cottage Grove Avenue, beyond Thirty-Third Street, and is built upon land given by the late Senator Douglas. Though established but about ten years, it now ranks as one of the leading universities of the Northwest, and is rapidly acquiring all the essentials of a complete institution.

THE DEARBORN OBSERVATORY.

This forms the Astronomical Department of the University. Its objects are to make original researches in Astronomical Science, to assist in the application of Astronomy to Geography, and other useful objects, and to furnish instruction in Astronomy to the students of the University, both those in the regular course and those who wish to give special attention to the study.

The principal instrument of the Observatory, at present, is the great Equatorial Refractor, by Alvan Clark and Sons, of Cambridge. Mass., the largest telescope in this country. This instrument is placed in the Dearborn Tower, built by the munificence of the Hon. J. Young Scammon, LL.D. The dimensions of the Equatorial are :

Diameter of Declination Circle, 30 inches.
Diameter of Hour Circle, 22 inches.
Focal Length of Object Glass, 23 feet.
Aperture of Object Glass, $18\frac{1}{2}$ inches.

The circles are read by two microscopes each, the hour circle to seconds of time, and the declination circle to ten seconds of space. The Observatory has also a chronometer (Wm. Bond and Son. No. 279), and a small astronomical library.

A meridian circle of the first class has been constructed by those eminent artists, Messrs. A. Repsold and Sons, of Hamburg, and is now on its way to Chicago. This instrument has a telescope of six French inches aperture, and divided circles of forty inches diameter; otherwise it is like Bessel's celebrated Konigsberg circle, by the same makers, with some late improvements in the illumination of the field and the wires, and with apparatus for recording declinations, a new invention of the makers.

ACADEMY OF SCIENCES.

THE Academy of Sciences is situated on the rear of lot No. 263 Wabash Avenue, between Van Buren and Jackson Streets. The building, which was finished early the present year, is fifty-five feet by fifty, fire-proof, and very strongly built, though plain in external appearance, as it will eventually form only an adjunct to a larger and finer building to be erected on the front of the lot, which is owned by the Academy. The first two stories contain the library, work rooms, offices, etc., while the upper story forms the museum, which is twenty-eight feet high, and surrounded by two galleries. The Academy was organized on its present basis in 1865. The nucleus of the collection of Natural History was furnished by the Smithsonian Institution, from the rich results of the Arctic Explorations of the late Major Kennicott. The collection was partially destroyed by fire in 1866, but the losses have been since more than made up. A considerable portion of the specimens has been allowed to remain packed in the store rooms of the Academy, as it was found that those displayed in the cases suffered greatly from the dampness which still exudes from the thick walls of the building.

CHICAGO WATER WORKS.

THE Water Works consist of the Pumping Works, the Lake Tunnel, and the Distributing Pipes.

The machinery for pumping consists of three engines and pumps, capable of delivering respectively 18,000,000, 12,000,000, and 8,000,000 gallons of water daily. Only two of the engines are ever worked at a time, it being necessary to hold one in reserve for repairs.

The engine house, when completed, will be about 150 feet long. The main portion, or center of the building, and the north wing, are now in use. They are of Athens marble, in the castelated style, and, together with the Water Tower, present an imposing appearance from the neighboring streets. The Water Tower is about 160 feet high, and contains a stand pipe about 140 feet high, and three feet in diameter. The object of the tower is to protect the stand pipe, which itself serves as a safety valve to the pumps.

The entire cost of the Pumping Works, Lake Tunnel, Water Tower, and connections, when completed, will be a little short of one million of dollars.

The Chicago Lake Tunnel was constructed in order to obtain water not affected by the impurities of the river, which at times used to render the supply exceedingly offensive. The shore water was often rendered very turbid by the northeasterly winds; but except when the storms are very protracted, the water now used by the city is clear.

The Tunnel is two miles long, five feet wide, and five feet two inches high, internal dimensions. The lining is brick masonry, about nine inches thick, laid in hydraulic cement. The entrance to the outer end of the tunnel is through a cast iron shaft, nine feet interior diameter, and two and a quarter inches thick, originally made in seven sections, each nine feet long. This shaft is provided with two gates, near its top, for admitting or excluding the water, and is protected from injury by a pentagonal breakwater or crib. This crib measures about fifty-eight feet on a side, externally, and has an open well of about thirty feet diameter, within; the thickness of the wall between the well and the outside of the crib being twenty-five feet. It consists of a very heavy frame of timber, filled in with loose stone. About one-quarter of the tunnel was excavated and lined from this end, and the remainder from the shore shaft, near the Pumping Works. The whole work was constructed in three years. The tunnel was calculated to deliver 54,000,000 U. S. gallons daily, under a head of 18 feet, or enough to supply one million of inhabitants with more than the average rate of consumption at the time the work was commenced. Actual experience shows that it is capable of doing more.

ARTESIAN WELL.

THE Artesian Well, at the Western Limits of the city, near Chicago Avenue, is about seven hundred feet deep, and nearly five inches in diameter, through limestone, and discharges daily upwards of half a million gallons of very clear, palatable water, having a very slight taste and odor of sulphur, and said to contain about fifty-six grains of solid matter to the U. S. gallon. There are really two wells here, very near together, the first was about four inches in diameter, and was bored for the purpose of finding oil. It was supposed that the second well would produce a corresponding increase in the discharge of the water, but though there was a decided increase, it did not meet previous expectation. Observations made with a pressure gauge, when the mouth of the well was stopped — rather imperfectly — show that the sources of this water must be at least one hundred feet above the lake, and probably much more.

At the Union Stock Yards, a little south of the Southern Limits, there is another Artesian Well, upwards of one thousand feet deep, affording a very copious supply of water.

THE BOARD OF TRADE,

THE HISTORICAL SOCIETY'S BUILDING AND COLLECTION,

THE RUSH MEDICAL COLLEGE.

THE WASHINGTON STREET TUNNEL.

THE STOCK YARDS,

THE COURT HOUSE AND ITS OBSERVATORY.

FLINT AND THOMPSON'S ELEVATORS.

PROGRAMME

WEDNESDAY, AUGUST 5th, 1868.

MORNING.

1. Opening of the Meeting by Dr. NEWBERRY, the retiring President, who will introduce Dr. B. A. GOULD, President of the Association for the Chicago Meeting.

2. Prayer by the Rev. Dr. R. W. PATTERSON.

3. Address of Welcome to the Association, by Hon. J. Y. SCAMMON, Chairman of the Local Committee.

4. Reply to the Address of Welcome, by President GOULD.

5. Election of Members to fill the Standing Committee.

6. Organization of the Sections.

7. Reading of Papers in the General and Sectional Meetings.

EVENING.

8. Entertainment at the Tremont House, at half-past eight, given by JOHN B. DRAKE, Esq.

1. On the Application of Electricity to the Maintenance of the Vibrations of the Tuning-fork : and of the Tuning-fork to the Excitement of Vibrations in Cords and Threads.

    By JOSEPH LOVERING.

2. On the Leaves of Coniferous Plants. By THOMAS MEEHAN.

3. On the Genus of extinct Sea-Saurians. *Elasmosaurus.*

    By EDWARD D. COPE.

4. On the Geology of the Mississippi Delta, and the Salt Deposit of Petite Anse.   By EUGENE W. HILGARD.

5. On the Theory of Luminous Hydrocarbon Flames.

    By EUGENE W. HILGARD.

6. On the Artistic Evidence of the Remote Colonization of the North-Western or American Continent by Maritime People of Distinct Nationalities before the Modern Era.

    By J. H. GIBBON.

7. Effect of Atmospheric Changes on the Eruptions of the great Geyser of Iceland.   By P. A. CHADBOURNE.

8. On the Action of Light upon Bromate and Iodide of Silver.

    By M. C. LEA.

9. Notes on the Defects of Lightning Rods.

    By JAMES BUSHER.

10. On the Boulder Field in Cedar County, Iowa.

    By RUSH EMERY.

11. Steam Boilers and the Various Causes assigned for their Explosions. Illustrated by Facts, Drawings and Experiments.   By JOSEPH A. MILLER.

12. Phases of Glacial Action in Maine at the Close of the Drift Period.   By N. T. TRUE.

13. Some Experiments on the Influence of the Physical Condition upon the Personal Equation, in Transit Observations.

    By W. A. ROGERS.

1. JOSEPH LOVERING, Professor, Cambridge, Mass. — Sherman House.

2. FRANKLIN B. HOUGH, Statistician, Lowville, N. Y.

3. CHARLES WHITTLESEY, Geological and Mining Eng., Cleveland, O.

4. JOHN L. HAYES, Secretary Nat. Assoc. of Wool Growers, Cambridge, Mass.

5. THEO. GILL, Librarian of Smithsonian Institute, Washington, D. C. — Wm. A. Doggett, Esq., 316 Michigan Ave.

6. W. CHAUVENET, Professor, St. Louis — Alex. Officer, Esq.

7. JAMES W. HARRIS, Asst. Sec. of the Assoc., Cambridge, Mass. — Orient House.

8. LOUIS FEUCHTWANGER, Chemist and Mineralogist, New York — Sherman House. Room 40.

9. A. B. ENGSTROM, Artist, Burlington, N. J.—Sherman House.

10. HENRY L. EUSTIS, Professor, Cambridge, Mass.—Sherman House.

11. CLEVELAND ABBE, Astronomer, Cincinnati, Ohio — S. C. Griggs, Esq., 204 Michigan Ave.

12. HORACE McMURTRIE, Engineer, Boston, Mass.— Sherman House.

13. O. N. ADAMS, Naturalist, LaSalle, Ill.

14. JOSEPH P. ROCKWELL, Mining Engineer, New Haven, Conn.

15. ALFRED P. ROCKWELL, Prof. of Mining, New Haven, Conn. — returned home.

16. B. A. GOULD, Astronomer, Cambridge, Mass. — E. B. McCagg, Esq.

17. J. C. WINSLOW, Physician, Danville, Ill. — Dr. Pierce, 323 West Randolph.

18. WM. J. BEAL, Professor, Union Springs, N. Y. — Mrs. Francis, 270 Wabash Ave.

19. JAMES HYATT, Naturalist, Bangall, N. Y. — Sherman House. Room 119.

20. JOSEPH KIRKLAND, Coal Miner, Danville, Ill. — 157 North Dearborn Street.

PROGRAMME

THURSDAY, AUGUST 6th, 1868.

MORNING.

General Session in Library Hall at Ten o'clock.

Meetings of the Sections in their Halls in Metropolitan Block, at One o'clock.

EVENING.

Eulogy on ALEXANDER DALLAS BACHE, by President GOULD, at Library Hall, at Half-past Seven o'clock.

Entertainment to be given the Members of the Association, their Ladies and Friends, at the house of WM. E. DOGGETT, Esq., 316 Michigan Avenue, at Nine o'clock. To this entertainment the Members of the Academy of Sciences are invited.

NOTICES.

Several of our Railway companies having, in aid of scientific investigation, generously offered to grant to Members of the Association passes to points of interest on their respective lines, the Local Committee would suggest that any Members of the Association who may desire to visit such points, which may be reached by railroads centering in Chicago, will hand their names to the Local Secretary, and the Committee will endeavor to procure passes for them.

The Members of the Association, with their ladies and friends, are invited by JAMES AITKEN, Esq., to visit the Opera House Art Gallery, and by Messrs. HOVEY & NICHOLS to visit their Art Gallery, at such times as may suit their individual convenience — the "Member's ticket" securing admission.

SECTION A.

MATHEMATICS, PHYSICS, AND CHEMISTRY.

Meeting in Caledonian Hall.

Chairman.

Prof. WM. CHAUVENET, of St. Louis.

Secretary.

Prof. GEO. F. BARKER, of New Haven.

Sectional Committee.

Prof. T. H. SAFFORD, of Chicago.
Prof. BENJ. SILLIMAN, of New Haven.
Prof. E. N. HORSFORD, of Cambridge.

TITLES OF PAPERS

For Thursday, August 6, 1868, in Section A.

1. A New Formula for the Reduction of Observations in the Prime Vertical, analagous to the Formula for the Reduction of Meridian Observations. By W. A. Rogers.
2. The Statics of the Four Types of Modern Chemistry, with Special Regard to the Water Type $\begin{smallmatrix} || \\ || \end{smallmatrix} \begin{smallmatrix} | \\ | \end{smallmatrix}$ O
   By Gustavus Hinrichs.
3. On the Chemico-Geological Relations of the Metals.
   By T. S. Hunt.
4. Some New Facts and Views concerning Aluminum.
   By Henry Wurtz.

5. Influence of the Moon upon the Weather. By ELIAS LOOMIS.

6. The Recent Contributions of Science to the Arts of Dyeing and Printing Woolen Tissues.   By JOHN L. HAYES.

7. Meteorolites from Mexico and Poland.

By LOUIS FEUCHTWANGER.

8. On the Combining Power of the Chemical Elements.

By S. D. TILLMAN.

9. Some Experiments on the Influence of the Physical Condition upon the Personal Equation, in Transit Observations.

By W. A. ROGERS.

10. On a Suspected Unknown Element in the Laurentian Magnetites.   By HENRY WURTZ.

11. The Calculation of the Crystalline Form of the Anhydrous Carbonates, Nitrates, Sulphates, Perchlorates, Permanganates, and other Salts of the Composition $A B_3 C$, or $A B_4 C$.   By GUSTAVUS HINRICHS.

SECTION B.

GEOLOGY AND NATURAL HISTORY.

MEETING IN THE ACADEMY HALL.

Chairman.

PROF. J. D. WHITNEY, OF CAMBRIDGE. MASS.

Secretary.

PROF. E. D. COPE, OF PHILADELPHIA, PA.

Sectional Committee.

A. H. WORTHEN, OF SPRINGFIELD, ILL.

PROF. O. C. MARSH, OF NEW HAVEN, CONN.

PROF. THEO. GILL, OF WASHINGTON, D. C.

17

TITLES OF PAPERS

For Thursday, August 6, 1868, in Section B.

1. On the Leaves of Coniferous Plants. By Thomas Meehan.
2. On the Geology of the Mississippi Delta, and the Salt Deposit of Petite Anse. By Eugene W. Hilgard.
3. Effect of Atmospheric Changes on the Eruptions of the great Geyser of Iceland. By P. A. Chadbourne.
4. On the Boulder Field in Cedar County, Iowa. By Rush Emery.
5. Supplementary Notes on Gold-Genesis. By Henry Wurtz.
6. Upon the Ammonoosac Gold Field in New Hampshire. By Henry Wurtz.
7. On Gold in the Laurentian Rocks of Canada. By T. S. Hunt.
8. On the Gold Region of Nova Scotia. By T. S. Hunt.
9. Origin of the Prairies. By J. W. Foster.
10. Exhibition of the Crania of Boötherium and Castoroides, with Remarks on their Geological Position and their Living Analogues. By J. W. Foster.
11. On the Stratigraphical Relations of the Fossil Horse in the United States. By Charles Whittlesey.
12. Brief Remarks on the Botany, Meteorology, and Geology of Mount Mansfield, Vermont. By James Hyatt.
13. The Habitable Features of the North American Continental Plateau near the Line of 35° Parallel North Latitude; containing a General Summary of Conclusions derived from a Review of its Aboriginal Population and Natural Features. By C. C. Parry.
14. Description of a New Species of *Protichnites* from the Potsdam Sandstone of New York. By O. C. Marsh.
15. The Progress and Present Condition of the Geological Survey of California. By J. D. Whitney.
16. The Quebec Group in Northern New Hampshire. By C. H. Hitchcock.
17. On the Geological Age and Equivalents of the Marshall Group. By A. Winchell.
18. Further Notice of Experiments on Snow and Ice at a Temperature below 32° F By Edward Hungerford.

21. JOHN DAVIS, Professor, Philadelphia, Pa.

22. JOHN WOODS, Philadelphia, Pa.

23. J. L. GRIMES, Lawyer, New York.

24. GUSTAVUS HINRICHS, Professor, Iowa City.

25. BENJ. SMITH LYMAN, Mining Eng., Philadelphia, Pa.

26. JOHN G. MORRIS, Professor of Zoölogy, Baltimore — Farwell House.

27. E. A. DALRYMPLE, Professor, Baltimore — Sherman House.

28. GEORGE A. LEAKIN, Baltimore — Sherman House.

29. J. H. GIBBON, Physician, North Carolina — Sherman House.

30. SAMUEL D. TILLMAN, Secretary of American Institute, New York — Tremont House.

31. SIMON NEWCOMB, Professsor of Mathematics, United States Observatory, Washington.

32. CHAS. AMES SPENCER, Professor Polytechnic Inst., Brooklyn.

33. WILLIAM A. ROGERS, Professor of Mathematics, Alfred University, Alfred Center, N.Y.

34. WILLIAM SAUNDERS, Chemist, London, Canada — St. James' Hotel.

35. NATH. T. TRUE, Geologist and Mineralogist, Bethel, Me.— Farwell House, 140 Madison Street.

36. B. SILLIMAN, Chemist, New Haven, Conn. — Mrs. Payson, cor. Clark and McCagg Streets.

37. EDWARD D. COPE, Professor, Philadelphia, Pa.

38. SAMUEL W. HILL, Geologist and Mining Engineer, Lake Superior, Mich.

39. E. N. HORSFORD, Chemist, Cambridge, Mass. — William E. Doggett, Esq., 316 Michigan Avenue.

40. JAMES H. EATON, Prof. Nat. Sci., Beloit, Wis. — Sherman House.

41. THEO. C. HILGARD, Physician, St. Louis — 484 Hubbard St.

42. EUG. W. HILGARD, Professor of Chemistry, Oxford, Miss. — 484 Hubbard Street.

43. H. C. Bolton, Student of Chemistry, New York — Sherman House.

44. Benj. C. Jillson, Professor of Chemistry, Pittsburg — Farwell House.

45. J. D. Whitney, Professor of Geology, Cambridge, Mass. — Sherman House.

46. W. D. Whitney, Professor of Linguistics, New Haven — Geo. G. Cook, Esq., Wabash Avenue.

47. Geo. W. Hough, Director of Dudley Observatory, Albany, N.Y. — Sherman House.

48. H. A. Newton, Professor of Mathematics, New Haven, Conn.

49. Chas. A. Joy, Professor of Chemistry, Columbia College, New York — Prof. Wheeler, 605 Michigan Avenue.

50. Edward W. Root, Professor of Chemistry, Hamilton College, Clinton, N.Y. — Sherman House.

51. Amasa McCoy, Professor, Chicago.

52. John Foster, Professor of Natural Philosophy, Union College, Schenectady, N.Y.

53. Charles U. Shepard, Jr., Professor of Chemistry, Medical College of South Carolina — Returned home.

54. J. S. Copes, President of New Orleans Academy of Sciences, New Orleans — Wm. E. Doggett, Esq., 316 Michigan Avenue.

55. George Little, State Geologist of Mississippi, Oxford, Miss.

56. A. N Prentiss, Professor of Botany and Horticulture, Lansing Mich.

57. O. C. Marsh, Professor of Palæontology, New Haven, Conn.

58. George F. Barker, Professor of Physics and Chemistry, New Haven, Conn.

59. Arthur W. Wright, Professor of Physics and Chemistry, Williamstown, Mass.

60. Eugene S. Bristol, Chemist, New Haven, Conn.

61. Herman A. Hagen, Entomologist, Cambridge, Mass. — Hon. J. Y. Scammon, 209 Michigan Av.

62. Edward Hungerford, Professor of Geology, Burlington, Vt.

63. CHAS. A. WHITE, State Geologist of Iowa, Iowa City. Iowa — Farwell House.

64. C. C. PARRY, Physician, Davenport, Iowa.

65. RUSH EMERY. Adj. Professor of Chemistry and Physics. Iowa City, Iowa.

66. THOS. MEEHAN, Professor of Botany, Philadelphia.

67. A. J. COOK, Professor of Zoology, Agricultural College. Lansing, Mich. — 127 Third Avenue.

68. E. F. HOBART, Professor of Natural History, Beloit, Wis.

69. J. L. SMITH, Professor of Chemistry, Louisville, Ky.

70. JOHN E. DAVIES, Professor of Chemistry, Madison, Wis.— 1582 Indiana Avenue.

71. JOHN COLLETT, Farmer, Eugene, Ind. — Tremont House.

72. JOSEPH F. TUTTLE, President of Wabash College, Crawfordsville, Ind. — Tremont House.

73. S. H. THOMPSON, Professor of Mathematics, Hanover College, Jefferson Co., Ind. — Tremont House.

74. W. D. HENKLE, Superintendent of Public Schools, Salem, Ohio — Tremont House.

75. B. W. McLAIN, Teacher of Natural Science, Fort Wayne, Ind. — Briggs House.

76. WM. M. CANBY, Professor of Botany, Wilmington, Del.— Tremont House.

77. WM. C. WHITFORD, Professor of Natural Science, Milton — Farwell House.

78. P. A. CHADBOURNE, President of the University of Wisconsin, Madison, Wis. — 476 Fulton Street.

79. DANIEL READ, President of State University of Missouri, Columbia, Mo.— Sherman House.

80. W. W. DANIELS, Professor of Agriculture, Madison, Wis. — Revere House.

81. ISAAC FERRIS, Chan. Univ., New York City, New York — L. Viele, Esq., 446 W. Jackson Street.

82. A. H. WORTHEN, State Geologist of Illinois, Springfield, Ill. — Chas. Knickerbocker, Esq., 1141 Michigan Avenue.

83. PHILIP T. TYSON, Geologist, Baltimore—504 West Lake.

84. JOHN. E. CLARK, Professor of Mathematics and Astronomy, Antioch College, Yellow Spa, Ohio.

85. GEO. F. MAGOUN, President of Iowa College, Grinnell, Iowa—P. L. Underwood, 526 Wabash Avenue.

Programme

for

FRIDAY, AUGUST 7th, 1868.

The General Session and meetings of the Sections will be held in the First Baptist Church.

Morning.

In the General Session the "Antiquity of Man" will be under discussion, and several Papers will be read upon the subject.

The rooms selected for the meetings of the Sections will be announced at the close of the General Session.

Evening.

Entertainment at the house of Dr. N. S. Davis, 797 Wabash Avenue.

STANDING COMMITTEE.

Dr. B. A. GOULD.
Col. CHARLES WHITTLESEY.
Prof. JOSEPH LOVERING.
Prof. SIMON NEWCOMB.
Prof. H. L. EUSTIS.
Prof. F. A. P. BARNARD.
Prof. S. D. TILLMAN.

Prof. J. S. NEWBERRY.
Prof. WOLCOTT GIBBS.
Prof. C. S. LYMAN.
Dr. A. L. ELWYN.
Prof. E. H. NEWTON.
Dr. C. C. PARRY.
Dr. J. H. RAUCH.

ADVISORY COMMITTEE

Chosen to unite with Standing Committee in the Nomination of Officers.

Section A.

Prof. ELIAS LOOMIS, of New Haven.
Prof. CLEVELAND ABBE, of Cincinnati.
Prof. J. C. WATSON, of Ann Arbor.
Prof. G. W. HOUGH, of Albany.

Section B.

Prof. E. A. DALRYMPLE, of Baltimore.
Prof. O. C. MARSH, of New Haven.
Dr. C. A. WHITE, of Iowa City.
Col. J. W. FOSTER, of Chicago.

SUB-COMMITTEES of the STANDING COMMITTEE.

1. *Committee on Nominations:*

H. L. EUSTIS.   C. C. PARRY.

2. *Committee on Papers:*

J. S. NEWBERRY   E. H. NEWTON.

3. *Committee on Hours and Business:*

J. H. RAUCH.   JOSEPH LOVERING.

NOTICES.

The meetings of the Association and its Sections will hereafter be held at the First Baptist Church on Wabash Avenue, south of Hubbard Court.

Omnibuses run on Wabash Avenue and cars on State Street. Passengers wishing to attend the meetings should stop at Hubbard Court.

The members of the Association, with those who are entertaining them, and the Members of the Academy of Sciences, are invited to an excursion on the Lake on Saturday afternoon. The Steamer will leave the dock (which will be named in to-morrow's Programme) punctually at three o'clock. A lunch will be provided on board. Member's tickets will entitle holders and their friends to admission on board.

The attention of those recently elected members is called to the following: " The admission fee of new members is five dollars, in addition to the annual subscription, which, including the price of the Proceedings, is three dollars for all members. These dues should be paid at as early a period as possible. They will be received by the Permanent Secretary, at the office of the Local Committee. According to Rule 21 of the Constitution, no person shall be considered a member until the dues for the meeting are paid."

The Secretaries of the Sections and other officers who have matter for publication in the " Programme," are requested to hand it in to the Local Secretary, daily, at as early an hour as possible.

Letters for members of the Association will hereafter be found at the office of the Local Committee, at the Sherman House.

On Monday evening next, an entertainment will be given to the Association by the the Chairman of the Local Committee.

SECTION A.

MATHEMATICS, PHYSICS, AND CHEMISTRY.

Chairman.

PROF. WM. CHAUVENET, OF ST. LOUIS.

Secretary.

PROF. GEO. F. BARKER, OF NEW HAVEN.

Sectional Committee.

PROF. T. H. SAFFORD, OF CHICAGO.
PROF. BENJ. SILLIMAN, OF NEW HAVEN.
PROF. E. N. HORSFORD, OF CAMBRIDGE.

TITLES OF PAPERS

For Friday, August 7, 1868, in Section A.

1. The Calculation of the Crystalline Form of the Anhydrous Carbonates, Nitrates, Sulphates, Perchlorates, Permanganates, and other Salts of the Composition $A B_3 C$, or $A B_4 C$. **By GUSTAVUS HINRICHS.** [30 minutes.]

2. Further Notice of Experiments on Snow and Ice at a Temperature below 32° F.
   By EDWARD HUNGERFORD. [30 m.]

3. On Hausen's Theory of the Physical Constitution of the Moon.
   By SIMON NEWCOMB. [10 m.]

4. The Resuscitation of the Cincinnati Observatory.
   By CLEVELAND ABBE. [15 m.]

5. On the Mathematical Investigations made for the Construction of the Illinois and St. Louis Bridge.

By WILLIAM CHAUVENET. [20 m.]

6. The Source of Free Hydrochloric Acid in the Gastric Juice.

By E. N. HOSFORD. [15 m.]

7. Remarks on the Galvanic Battery.

By G. W. HOUGH. [30 m.]

8. On a proposed new Mechanism for the study of Galvanic Batteries. By G. W. HOUGH. [30 m.]

9. Phosphoric Acid a Constituent of Butter.

By E. N. HORSFORD. [10 m.]

10. The Hot Term of July. By O. N. STODDARD. [15 m.]

SECTION B.

GEOLOGY AND NATURAL HISTORY.

Chairman.

PROF. J. D. WHITNEY, OF CAMBRIDGE, MASS.

Secretary.

PROF. E. D. COPE, OF PHILADELPHIA, PA.

Sectional Committee.

A. H. WORTHEN, OF SPRINGFIELD, ILL.
PROF. O. C. MARSH, OF NEW HAVEN, CONN.
PROF. THEO. GILL, OF WASHINGTON, D. C.

TITLES OF PAPERS

For Friday. August 7, 1868, in Section B.

1. On Gold in the Laurentian Rocks of Canada.
   By T. S. HUNT.

2. On the Gold Region of Nova Scotia.   By T. S. HUNT.

3. On the Upper Silurian and Devonian Rocks of Ontario.
   By T. S. HUNT.

4. Origin of the Prairies.   By J. W. FOSTER.

5. On the Geological Age and Equivalents of the Marshall Group.   By A. WINCHELL.

6. Notice of Some New Vertebrate Remains from the Tertiary of New Jersey.   By O. C. MARSH.

7. On the Plasticity of Rocks, and origin of the Structure of the so-called Grave Stone Slates of California.
   By W. P. BLAKE.

8. Source of Muscular Power.   By E. N. HORSFORD.

9. Relations of the Metamorphoses of the Phosphates of Waste and Repair.   By E. N. HORSFORD.

10. Fluorine a Constituent of the Brain.   By E. N. HORSFORD.

11. On the Physical Geography of the Continent of North America during the different Geological Periods.
    By J. S. NEWBERRY.

12. Fuel Resources of Illinois.   By A. H. WORTHEN.

13. Geological Section of Ohio.   By E. B. ANDREWS.

29. Influence of the Moon upon the Weather. By ELIAS LOOMIS.
30. On Some Points in the Geology of Vermont.
      By T. S. HUNT.
31. On the Upper Silurian and Devonian Rocks of Ontario.
      By T. S. HUNT.
32. On Gold in the Laurentian Rocks of Canada.
      By T. S. HUNT.
33. On the Gold Regions of Nova Scotia.
      By T. S. HUNT.
34. On the Chemico-Geological Relations of the Metals.
      By T. S. HUNT.
35. The Antiquity of Man in North America.
      By J. W. FOSTER.
36. Origin of the Prairies.   By J. W. FOSTER.
37. Exhibition of the Crania of Boötherium and Castoroides,
      with Remarks on their Geological Position and their
      Living Analogues.   By J. W. FOSTER.
38. On the Occurrence of Fluor Spar in Southern Illinois.
      By J. W. FOSTER.
39. On the Refrigeration of Continents.   By J. W. FOSTER.
40. On the Occurrence of Tin in Missouri. By J. W. FOSTER.
41. Migrations of the Indian Family.   By L. H. MORGAN.
42. The Application of Carbonic Acid Gas, in the Extinguish-
      ment of Fire.   By E. L. BUTTRICK.
43. Hough's Barometrograph as applied to the Investigation of
      the Storm Curve.   By J. H. COFFIN.
44. Brief Remarks on the Botany, Meteorology, and Geology of
      Mount Mansfield, Vermont.   By JAMES HYATT.
45. Habits and Peculiarities of Plants in South Eastern New
      York and Vicinity.   By JAMES HYATT.
46. Movements in Stratified Rocks, since the Glacial Epoch.
      By JAMES HYATT.
47. On the Stratigraphical Relations of the Fossil Horse in the
      United States.   By CHARLES WHITTLESEY.
48. Abstract of the Geological Evidences of Man's Antiquity in
      the United States.   By CHARLES WHITTLESEY.

68. Atomic Motion. By H. F. Walling.
69. On the Mathematical Investigations made for the Construction of the Illinois and St. Louis Bridge.
By William Chauvenet.
70. On a Method of Measuring very Small Rectilinear Motions.
By William Chauvenet.
71. The Source of Free Hydrochloric Acid in the Gastric Juice.
By E. N. Horsford.
72. Relations of the Metamorphoses of the Phosphates to Waste and Repair. By E. N. Horsford.
73. Economy in the Conversion of Beef into Food.
By E. N. Horsford.
74. Remarks on the Galvanic Battery.
By G. W. Hough.
75. On a proposed new Mechanism for the study of Galvanic Batteries. By G. W. Hough.
76. Remarks on the total Disturbance of the Barometrical Column. By G. W. Hough.
77. Announcement of the Discovery of Cretaceous Rocks in Guthrie County, Iowa. By C. A. White.
78. Remarks upon the redquartzite Boulders and their Original Ledges *in situ* in Northwestern Iowa, Eastern Dakota, and Southwestern Minnesota. By C. A. White.
79. The Principles of Statistics as applied to the Census.
By F. B. Hough.
80. On the Geological Age and Equivalents of the Marshall Group. By A. Winchell.
81. Exhibition of a New Geological Chart. By A. Winchell.
82. Exhibition of a New Label Holder for Zoölogical Specimens.
By A. Winchell.
83. On some Points in Geological Nomenclature.
By A. Winchell.
84. The Profiles of Blast Furnaces. By Thomas Egleston.
85. Phosphoric Acid a Constituent of Butter.
By E. N. Horsford.
86. Source of Muscular Power. By E. N. Horsford.
87. Fluorine a Constituent of the Brain. By E. N. Horsford.
88. Fossil Fishes, Insects, Crustacea, etc., of the Coal Measures of Grundy County, Illinois. By A. H. Worthen.
89. Fuel Resources of Illinois. By A. H. Worthen.

ARRIVALS.

86. CARL VON COELLEN, Professor of Mathematics, Iowa College, Grinnell, Iowa—P. L. Underwood, 526 Wabash Avenue.

87. A. S. PACKARD Jr., Professor of Natural History, Peabody Academy, Salem, Mass—Sherman House.

88. F. A. P. BARNARD, President of Columbia College, New York City.—Sherman House.

89. O. H. FITCH, Lawyer, Ashtabula, Ohio—Sherman House.

90. EDWARD H. FITCH, Lawyer, Ashtabula, Ohio—Sherman House.

91. W. H. BULLOCH, Optician, Chicago—147 Madison Street.

92. H. F. WALLING, Professor of Civil Engineering, Lafayette College, Brooklyn N. Y.—Farwell House.

93. J. N. STOCKWELL, Mathematician, Brecksville, Ohio—Farwell House.

94. E. S. CARR, Professor of Chemistry, Madison Wis.

95. H. M. BANNISTER, Ph. B, Assist. Illinois Geological Survey, Evanston, Cook Co., Ill.

96. Rev. EDWARD C. BOLLES, Secretary of the Portland Society of Natural History, Portland, Me.—168 Michigan Avenue.

97. A. WINCHELL, Professor of Geology, Zoölogy, and Botany, Ann Arbor, Mich.

98. T. STERRY HUNT, of the Geological Survey of Canada, Montreal—342 North Lasalle Street.

99. WM. P. BLAKE, Professor of Mineralogy and Geology, California—Sherman House.

100. JAMES HALL, New York State Geologist, Albany, N.Y.

101. T. A. MEYSENBURG, Civil Engineer, St. Louis, Mo.

102. JOEL HENDRICK, Professor of Latin and Greek Languages, Horellsville, N.Y.

103. JAMES C. WATSON, Astronomer, Ann Arbor, Mich.

104. CHAS. H. BRIGHAM, Professor of Ecclesiastical History, Meadville Theological School, Ann Arbor.

105. EDWARD DOUBLEDAY HARRIS, Architect, Cambridge, Mass.

106. CHAS. V. RILEY, State Entomologist, St. Louis, Mo.

107. JOHN H. KLIPPART, Ohio State Board of Agriculture, Columbus, Ohio — 67 Maple Street.

108. O. N. STODDARD, Professor of Natural Sciences, Miami University, Oxford, Ohio — Charles Paine, Esq., 342 N. Lasalle Street.

109. HERMAN HERZER, Minister of the Gospel, Columbus, Ohio.

110. JOSEPH MILLER, Civil Engineer, New York — Sherman House.

111. OLIVER EVERETT, Physician, Dixon, Ill.

112. CHAS. BILL, Publisher, Chicago, Ill.— Office, 132 S. Clark Street.

113. L. B. CASE, Geologist, Richmond, Ind.

114. EDWARD H. BEEBE, Miner, Galena — 368 Ohio Street.

115. ROSWELL PARK, D.D., Teacher, Chicago.

116. C. G. HAMMOND, Chicago — 272 Erie Street.

117. C. E. HUBBARD, Lawyer, Boston, Mass.

118. RODNEY WELCH, Professor of Chemistry, Chicago — 128 State Street.

119. OLIVER MARCY, Professor of Natural Sciences, North-Western University, Evanston, Ill.

120. S. H. PEABODY, Professor of Natural Science, Chicago High School, Chicago.

121. CHAS. J. SHEFFIELD, Chemist, Cleveland, Ohio.

122. LOUIS C. WURTZEL, Clergyman, Acton Vale, Prov. Quebec — 160 Fulton Street.

123. C. H. HITCHCOCK, Geologist, New York — Richmond House.

124. D. P. MAYHEW, Professor of Natural Science, Detroit — Richmond House.

125. ALBERT H. TUTTLE, Student of Natural History, Cleveland, O.

126. P. H. VANDER WEYDE, Professor of Natural Sciences, New York City — Sherman House.

127. J. BAKER EDWARDS, Consulting Chemist, Montreal — Farwell House.

128. E. B. ANDREWS, Professor of Geology, Marietta, O. — Sherman House.

129. P. R. HOY, Physician and Naturalist, Racine, Wis.

130. JOHN M. WOODWORTH, M.D., Surgeon, Chicago — Rooms 2 and 3, Lombard Block.

131. L. S. PENNINGTON, Professor of Horticulture and Agriculture, Sterling, Ill. — Joseph Bullock.

132. E. W. BLATCHFORD, Chicago — 375 N. LaSalle Street.

133. E. S. CHESBROUGH, Civil Engineer, Chicago — 317 N. LaSalle Street.

134. WALTER HAY, Physician, Chicago — 188 S. Sangamon Street.

135. ELIAS LOOMIS, Astronomer, New Haven — 189 Briggs House.

136. A. HAMMER, Professor of Surgery, St. Louis, Mo. — 175 N. Clark Street.

137. JOHN WOODS, Philadelphia.

138. JOHN DAVIS, Professor, Philadelphia.

139. JAMES S. JEWELL, Physician, Evanston, Ill.

140. THOS. D. ROBERTSON, Rockford.

141. J. S. NEWBERRY, Professor of Geology, New York — Col. C. G. Hammond, 272 Erie Street.

142. WM. WATSON, Professor of Engineering, Cambridge, Mass. — Sherman House.

143. BENJ. ALVORD, Brig. General, U.S.A., Omaha, Neb. — Dr. J. V. Z. Blaney, 136 N. State Street.

144. DAVENPORT FISHER, Chemist, Milwaukee, Wis. — Wm. H. Clarke, Esq., 57 W. Hinsdale Street.

145. WM. H. CLARKE, Civil Engineer, Chicago — 57 W. Hinsdale Street.

146. W. O. ATWATER, Assistant, Scientific School, Yale, New Haven, Conn. — Farwell House.

147. HARRISON ALLEN, Surgeon, Professor of Comparative Anatomy and Zoölogy, University of Penn., Philadelphia — Orrington Lunt, Esq.

148. HORATIO C. WOOD, Jr., Physician and Professor of Botany, University of Penn., Philadelphia.

149. BENJ. D. WALSH, Entomologist, Rock Island, Ill. —

150. D. H. COCHRAN, President of Brooklyn Polytechnic Inst., Brooklyn — Sherman House.

151. WM. EIMBECK, Civil Engineer, St. Louis, Mo. — Sherman House, room 190.

152. S. EDWARD WARREN, Prof. Rens., Polytechnic Inst., Troy, N. Y. — Sherman House.

153. DASCOM GREENE, Professor of Mathematics, etc., Troy N. Y.

Programme

for

SATURDAY, AUGUST 8th, 1868.

Morning.

The General Session will be held in Library Hall. The following Papers will be read:

1. Steam Boilers and the Various Causes assigned for their Explosions, illustrated by Facts, Drawings and Experiments.

   By Joseph A. Miller.

2. On the Application of Electricity to the Maintenance of the Vibration of the Tuning-fork, and of the Tuning-fork to the Excitement of Vibrations in Cords and Threads.

   By Joseph Lovering.

There will be no meetings of the Sections to-day.

Afternoon.

Excursion upon the Lake, from Goodrich's Dock, at half-past two o'clock.

STANDING COMMITTEE.

Dr. B. A. GOULD.
Col. CHARLES WHITTLESEY.
Prof. JOSEPH LOVERING.
Prof. SIMON NEWCOMB.
Prof. WILLIAM CHAUVENET.
Prof. H. L. EUSTIS.
Prof. F. A. P. BARNARD.
Prof. S. D. TILLMAN.

Prof. J. S. NEWBERRY.
Prof. WOLCOTT GIBBS.
Prof. C. S. LYMAN.
Dr. A. L. ELWYN.
Prof. J. D. WHITNEY.
Prof. H. E. NEWTON.
Dr. C. C. PARRY.
Dr. J. H. RAUCH.

ADDITIONAL MEMBERS

Chosen to unite with Standing Committee as a Council for the Nomination of Officers.

Section A.

Prof. ELIAS LOOMIS, of New Haven.
Prof. CLEVELAND ABBE, of Cincinnati.
Prof. J. C. WATSON, of Ann Arbor.
Prof. G. W. HOUGH, of Albany.

Section B.

Prof. E. A. DALRYMPLE, of Baltimore.
Prof. O. C. MARSH, of New Haven.
Dr. C. A. WHITE, of Iowa City.
Col. J. W. FOSTER, of Chicago.

SUB-COMMITTEES of the STANDING COMMITTEE.

1. *Committee on Nominations:*

H. L. EUSTIS.   C. C. PARRY.

2. *Committee on Papers:*

J. S. NEWBERRY.   H. E. NEWTON.

3. *Committee on Hours and Business:*

J. H. RAUCH.   JOSEPH LOVERING.

Music at Lincoln Park,

ON SATURDAY AFTERNOON.

1. March—Helene . . . . Winter
2. Stabat Mater . . . . Rossini
3. Concert Polka . . . . Labitzky
4. Overture—The Humor of Berlin . . Conradi
5. Waltz—Memories of Home . . . Vaas
6. Coronation March from "The Prophet" Meyerbeer
7. Festival Overture . . . Leutner
8. Gallop—Halloo, Halloo . Steinmüller
9. Fantasie from "Faust"—By request Gounond
10. Finale—National Airs . . . ———

Church, Goodman & Donnelley, Printers.

NOTICES.

The steamer *Orion* will leave Goodrich's Dock, just below Rush Street Bridge, on the south side of the river, at half-past two o'clock, for an excursion on the Lake. A lunch will be provided on board, and music from a quartette club may be expected. To this excursion the members of the Association and their friends, and the members of the Academy of Sciences, with ladies, are invited.

There will be Instrumental Music at Lincoln Park, after the return of the Excursionists, until half-past seven o'clock. Lincoln Park may be reached by the horse cars on North Clark Street.

On Monday evening next, an entertainment will be given to the Association by the Hon. J. YOUNG SCAMMON, Chairman of the Local Committee, at his residence, 209 Michigan Avenue, to which are invited, in addition to the Members of the Association, and their ladies and friends, the Members of the Academy of Sciences, the Historical Society, and the Astronomical Society, and the Faculties of the Universities and Medical Schools in Chicago and vicinity. Those who are entertaining Members of the Association, with their ladies, are also invited.

The Local Committee desire to state that at least twenty-four hours are required to procure passes on the railroads for those who wish to make excursions, and applications for them should be made as early as possible. The announcement in Thursday's Programme was made under the impression that the excursion passes would be required at the close of the session. The officers of the Railway Companies prefer to have applications for passes presented to them in the form of lists, at stated times, rather than singly, at all times. The Local Committee trust that this will be a sufficient apology to those who may have experienced delay in the reception of their passes.

---

90. On the Physical Geography of the Continent of North America during the different Geological Periods.

By J. S. NEWBERRY.

91. On the Transportation of the Materials forming the Carboniferous Conglomerates. By J. S. NEWBERRY.

92. On the Surface Geology of the Basin of the Great Lakes and the Upper Mississippi Valley. By J. S. NEWBERRY.

93. On the Plasticity of Rocks, and Origin of the Structure of the so-called Grave Stone Slates of California.

By W. P. BLAKE.

94. On the Gradual Dessication of the Western Portions of North America. By W. P. BLAKE.

95. Vestiges of Pre-historic Races in California.

By W. P. BLAKE.

96. Geological Section of Ohio. By E. B. ANDREWS.

97. The Hot Term of July. By O. N. STODDARD.

98. The Nature of Electric Discharge. By O. N. STODDARD.

99. The Higher Law of Correlation. By O. N. STODDARD.

100. On Certain Physical Features of the Mississippi River.

By G. K. WARREN.

101. The Vertebral Type of the Cranium a Quinary one.

By T. C. HILGARD.

102. Extremities of the Skeleton Typically 5.

By T. C. HILGARD.

103. The Quebec Group in Northern New Hampshire.

By C. H. HITCHCOCK.

104. The Supposed Triassic Foot-marks in Kansas.

By C. H. HITCHCOCK.

105. The Distortions of Pebbles in Conglomerate at Rangly. Maine. By G. L. VASE.

106. On *Elasmognathus* and its Relations to the Tapiridæ generally. By THEODORE GILL.

107. On the Classification and Relations of Seals.

By THEODORE GILL.

108. On the Secular Recurrence of Identical Petrogenetic Conditions. By A. WINCHELL.

109. Superficial Geology of the Lake Shore near Chicago. By J. S. JEWELL.

110. The Darwinian Theory of Development. By CHARLES MORAN.

111. The Periodic Law in the Failure of Harvests and Inundations, with Suggestions as to their Insurance. By GEORGE A. LEAKIN.

112. On the Old Lake Beds of the Prairie Region. By S. J. WALLACE.

113. On the Progress and Present Condition of the Geological Survey of California. By J. D. WHITNEY.

114. The Fossil Human Skull of Calaveras County, California. By J. D. WHITNEY.

115. Some Points in the Surface Geology of the Western Side of the American Continent. By J. D. WHITNEY.

116. The Yosemite Valley. By J. D. WHITNEY.

117. On the Structure and Aqueous Origin of Gold-bearing Mineral Veins. By BENJAMIN SILLIMAN.

118. On Methods of Amalgamation in the Treatment of Gold Ores. By BENJAMIN SILLIMAN.

119. On the Occurrence of the Mastodon in the Deep-Lying Gold Placers of California. By BENJAMIN SILLIMAN.

120. On the Relation between the Atomic Volume of Different Metals, and their Paramagnetic and Diamagnetic Properties. By P. H. VANDER WEYDE.

121. Geodes. By W. W. WILLIAMS.

122. Modern Discoveries in Palestine. By W. W. WILLIAMS.

123. On the Molecular Arrangement of the Inorganic Acids. By GEORGE F. BARKER.

124. Theory of the Prediction of Star Places. By T. H. SAFFORD.

125. Sketch of the Topography, Geology and Antiquities of the Caucasus. By F. VON KOSCHKULL.

126. On Two New Fossil Trees, the oldest known, found by Rev. H. HERZER, in the Devonian Rocks of Ohio. By J. S. NEWBERRY.

127. Remarks on the Secular Variations of the Eccentricities and Perihelia of the Eight Principal Planets. By J. S. STOCKWELL.

128. Description and Application of the Heliostat, and Method of Running True Meridian Lines in Surveying.

By MICHAEL W. McDERMOTT.

129. Report on Archæology and Ethnology. By W. DE HASS.

130. Archæology and Ethnology of the Mississippi Valley.

By W. DE HASS.

131. Tides in Lakes. By H. A. NEWTON.

132. On the Evaporative Power of the Sun near the Base of the Sierra Nevada, in Calaveras County, California.

By BENJAMIN SILLIMAN.

154. SIDNEY S. LYON. Geologist. Jeffersonville. Ind. — Sherman House.

155. EDWARD HITCHCOCK. Professor of Physics. Amherst. Mass. — Richmond House.

156. EDWIN POWELL. Physician. Chicago — 45 S. Clark Street.

157. H. C. FREEMAN. Mining Engineer and Geologist. South Pass. Ill.

158. M. HECKARD. Mining Engineer. Pomeroy, Ohio.

159. HENRY H. BABCOCK. Teacher. Chicago.

160. LEWIS H. MORGAN. Lawyer. Rochester — Sherman House.

161. ROBERT BROWN. Jr., Naturalist. Cincinnati. O. — Lyman Baird. Esq., 383 N. LaSalle Street.

162. GEORGE H. PERKINS. Zoölogist. New Haven. Con. — Kenwood.

163. N. S. DAVIS. Professor in the Chicago Medical College — 797 Wabash Avenue.

164. B. WATERHOUSE HAWKINS. Teacher of Palæontology. New York City.

165. H. A. JOHNSON. Professor and Physician. Chicago — 611 Wabash Avenue.

166. S. N. MANNING. Clergyman. Kankakee. Ill.

167. JOHN ROCKWELL. Superintendent of Coal Mine. LaSalle. Ill. — Wm. B. Ogden. Esq., cor. Rush and Ontario Streets.

168. JOHN MURRISH. Merchant. Mazomanee.

169. N. M. DODSON. Physician. Berlin. Wis.

170. WM. W. WILLIAMS. Clergyman and Editor. Winchester. Central Illinois — 688 Sedgwick Street.

171. SAMUEL STONE. Chicago — 612 N. Clark Street.

172. S. A. BRIGGS. Microscopist. Chicago.

173. D. READ. President of College. Upper Alton. Ill.

174. J. Y. SCAMMON. President of Chicago Astronomical Society. etc., etc. — 209 Michigan Avenue.

175. CHARLES MORAN, Banker, New York — Sherman House.

176. E. L. YOUMANS, Professor, New York.

177. ROBERT T. LINCOLN, Lawyer, Chicago.

178. U. H. CROSBY, Chicago.

179. JOHN A. WARDER, Farmer, Hamilton Co., Ohio — Sherman House.

180. CHARLES GRANT, Assistant Professor of Latin, Aberdeen, Scotland.

181. THOMAS EGLESTON, Professor of Mineralogy and Metallurgy, New York — Sherman House.

182. HENRY MILES, A.M., Secretary (Eng.) Department Pub. Instruction, Prov. Quebec, Quebec City.

183. JOSEPH TINGLEY, Professor of Natural Sciences, Greencastle, Ind.

184. WM. H. MYERS, Physician, Fort Wayne, Ind.

185. CLINTON ROOSEVELT, Lawyer, New York City.

186. WM. FERREL, Naut. Almanac and U. S. Coast Survey, Cambridge, Mass.

187. GEO. C. WALKER, President of Chicago Academy of Sciences, Chicago — 261 Michigan Avenue.

188. T. H. SAFFORD, Professor of Astronomy and Director of Dearborn Observatory.

189. FRANK H. BRADLEY, Assist. Geologist of Illinois — New Haven, Conn.

190. MICHEL McDERMOTT, Civil Engineer and City Surveyor.

191. P. J. FARNSWORTH, Physician, Clinton, Iowa — Briggs House.

192. A. S. WELCH, President of Iowa Agricultural College — Briggs House.

193. CHAS. KNICKERBOCKER, Engraver of Scientific Subjects, Chicago — 1141 Michigan Avenue.

194. JOHN H. RAUCH, Physician, Chicago — 140 Madison Street.

195. J. HIBBARD, Clergyman, Chicago — 70 Third Avenue.

196. W. A. P. DILLINGHAM, Clergyman, Augusta, Maine — Hon. J. Y. Scammon, 209 Michigan Avenue.

197. THOS. BASSNETT, Sec. Chicago and Montreal Telegraph Co., Ottawa, Ill. — Tremont House.

198. FRED. J. HUSE, Asst. Local Secretary, Evanston, Cook Co., Ill. — Sherman House.

Programme for Saturday Evening.

SECTION A.

MATHEMATICS, PHYSICS, AND CHEMISTRY.

Chairman.

PROF. WM. CHAUVENET, OF ST. LOUIS.

Secretary.

PROF. GEO. F. BARKER, OF NEW HAVEN.

Sectional Committee.

PROF. T. H. SAFFORD, OF CHICAGO.
PROF. BENJ. SILLIMAN, OF NEW HAVEN.
PROF. E. N. HORSFORD, OF CAMBRIDGE.

TITLES OF PAPERS

For Saturday, August 8, 1868, in Section A.

EVENING SESSION.

1. Phosphoric Acid a Constituent of Butter.
   By E. N. HORSFORD. [10 minutes.]
2. The Hot Term of July, 1868.
   By O. N. STODDARD. [15 m.]
3. The Principles of Statistics as applied to the Census.
   By F. B. HOUGH. [10 m.]
4. Remarks on the Galvanic Battery.
   By G. W. HOUGH. [10 m.]
5. On a proposed new Mechanism for the study of Galvanic
   Batteries. By G. W. HOUGH. [10 m.]

SECTION B.

GEOLOGY AND NATURAL HISTORY.

Chairman.
PROF. J. D. WHITNEY. OF CAMBRIDGE, MASS.

Secretary.
PROF. E. D. COPE. OF PHILADELPHIA, PA.

Sectional Committee.
A. H. WORTHEN. OF SPRINGFIELD. ILL.
PROF. O. C. MARSH, OF NEW HAVEN. CONN.
PROF. THEO. GILL. OF WASHINGTON. D. C.

TITLES OF PAPERS

For Saturday, August 8, 1868, in Section B.

EVENING SESSION.

1. Notice of some New Vertebrate Remains from the Tertiary of New Jersey.   By O. C. MARSH.
2. On the Plasticity of Rocks, and Origin of the Structure of the so-called Grave Stone Slates of California.
                                          By W. P. BLAKE.
3. Source of Muscular Power.   By E. N. HORSFORD.
4. Relations of the Metamorphoses of the Phosphates to Waste and Repair.   By E. N. HORSFORD.
5. Fluorine a Constituent of the Brain.   By E. N. HORSFORD.
6. On the Physical Geography of the Continent of North America during the different Geological Periods.
                                          By J. S. NEWBERRY.
7. Fuel Resources of Illinois.   By A. H. WORTHEN.
8. Geological Section of Ohio.   By E. B. ANDREWS.
9. On the Origin of Prairies.   By J. W. FOSTER.

ARRIVALS.

199. E. A. HILL, Electrician, Chicago.

200. DR. VON KOSCHKULL, Tiflis, Russia — Sherman House.

201. F. STALLKNECKT, New York — Sherman House.

202. R. PUMPELLY, Engineer of Mines, New York — Sherman House.

203. I. A. LAPHAM, Civil Engineer, Milwaukee — Col. Stone, 612 N. Clark Street.

204. JAMES BUSHIE, Professor, Worcester, Mass.

205. L. G. OLMSTEAD, Archæologist, Morran Station, N. Y.

206. M. L. HORSFORD, Cambridge.

207. DR. MANNHEIMER, Physician, Chicago.

208. E. L. LATHROP, Physician, Chicago.

209. Z. GROVER, Teacher, Chicago.

210. BENJAMIN DURHAM, Physician — 73 Twenty-fourth St., Chicago.

211. N. F. PECK, M.D., Davenport.

212. A. S. KEISSELL, late Superintendent Minneapolis Public Schools, Davenport.

213. JEROME ALLEN, Superintendent of Schools, Monticello, Ia. — 345 Calumet Avenue.

214. Mrs. S. A. HUBBARD, Kalamazoo, Mich.

215. S. C. GROVE, Portland, Me.

133. Proofs that the Changes of Climate and Dislocations and Upheavals of the Earth's Strata are due to Astronomical and not to Glacial Action.   By CLINTON ROOSEVELT.

134. The True Mode of Building Steam Vessels so as to secure the greatest speed possible.   By CLINTON ROOSEVELT.

135. The Scientific Mode of Anchoring Vessels in a gale on a lee shore, or to hold to a " drag" at sea.
By CLINTON ROOSEVELT.

136. The Beginning of Creation, of the Sun and Plants, with Strictures on the Cosmogonies of DesCartes, Kant and LaPlace.   By CLINTON ROOSEVELT.

137. On the Tides of Lake Michigan.   By W. FERREL.

138. On Redemption Periods of Monetary Values which involve Life Contingencies.   By E. B. ELLIOTT.

139. On the Metrical Unification of International Coinage.
By E. B. ELLIOTT.

140. A Few Facts concerning the Vital Statistics of Amherst College.   By EDWARD HITCHCOCK.

141. On the Archaeological Value of Certain Ancient Beads.
By L. G. OLMSTEAD.

142. Exhibition of a New Selenograph.   By JEROME ALLEN.

143. On a New Method of Measurement Map Drawing for Schools.   By JEROME ALLEN.

144. Glaciers as Extensive and Constant Geologic Agencies.
By JAMES HYATT.

145. Points in the Geology of Hudson River.
By JAMES HYATT.

146. On Some of the Causes which Affect the Rapidity of Erosion of Rocks and of River Valleys.
By WM. P. BLAKE.

147. On the Interpretation of Fossils.
By B. WATERHOUSE HAWKINS.

148. Notes on the Origin of Bitumens, together with Experiments upon the Formation of Asphaltum.   By S. F. PECKHAM.

149. Note on Epitrochoidal Teeth.   By WILLIAM WATSON.

PROGRAMME

MONDAY, AUGUST 10, 1868.

MORNING.

The General Session will be held in the Lecture Room of the First Baptist Church. The following Papers will be read :

1. The Fossil Human Skull of Calaveras County, California. By J. D. WHITNEY.

2. On the Artistic Evidence of the Remote Colonization of the Great Western or American Continent, by Maritime People of Distinct Nationalities before the Modern Era. By J. H. GIBBON.

To be followed by a Discussion on the Antiquity of Man.

The meetings of the Sections will be held in their respective rooms in the Church at two o'clock, P. M.

EVENING.

Entertainment given by the HON. J. YOUNG SCAMMON, at his residence, No. 209 Michigan Avenue.

STANDING COMMITTEE.

Dr. B. A. GOULD.
Col. CHARLES WHITTLESEY.
Prof. JOSEPH LOVERING.
Prof. SIMON NEWCOMB.
Prof. H. L. EUSTIS.
Prof. F. A. P. BARNARD.
Prof. S. D. TILLMAN.

Prof. J. S. NEWBERRY.
Prof. WOLCOTT GIBBS.
Prof. C. S. LYMAN.
Dr. A. L. ELWYN.
Prof. H. A. NEWTON.
Dr. C. C. PARRY.
Dr. J. H. RAUCH.

As Chairmen of the Sections:

SECTION A.

Prof. WILLIAM CHAUVENET.

SECTION B.

Prof. J. D. WHITNEY.

ADDITIONAL MEMBERS

Chosen to unite with Standing Committee as a Council for the Nomination of Officers.

SECTION A.

Prof. ELIAS LOOMIS, of New Haven.
Prof. CLEVELAND ABBE, of Cincinnati.
Prof. J. C. WATSON, of Ann Arbor.
Prof. G. W. HOUGH, of Albany.

SECTION B.

Prof. E. A. DALRYMPLE, of Baltimore.
Prof. O. C. MARSH, of New Haven.
Dr. C. A. WHITE, of Iowa City.
Col. J. W. FOSTER, of Chicago.

SUB-COMMITTEES of the STANDING COMMITTEE.

1. *Committee on Nominations:*

H. L. EUSTIS.   C. C. PARRY.

2. *Committee on Papers:*

J. S. NEWBERRY.   H. A. NEWTON.

3. *Committee on Hours and Business:*

J. H. RAUCH.   JOSEPH LOVERING.

The Local Committee would state that they have been thus far applied to for Passes over the North-Western Railroad only, while excursions of great interest may be made in several other directions. At Lasalle, on the Illinois Central Railroad, the Coal Measures are to be seen in contact with the Trenton Limestone. At Burlington, on the Chicago, Burlington and Quincy Railroad, may be found the Burlington Limestone, rich in crinoids. At Alton, on the Chicago, Alton and St. Louis Railroad, the Carboniferous Limestones are found in connection with the Coal Measures. Along the line of either of the above roads the Prairie country may be seen in its most perfect development.

This evening, an entertainment will be given to the Association by the Hon. J. YOUNG SCAMMON, Chairman of the Local Committee, at his residence, 209 Michigan Avenue, to which are invited, in addition to the Members of the Association, and their ladies and friends, the Members of the Academy of Sciences, the Historical Society, and the Astronomical Society, and the Faculties of the Universities and Medical Schools in Chicago and vicinity. Those who are entertaining Members of the Association, with their ladies, are also invited.

To-morrow (Tuesday) evening an entertainment will be given to the members of the Association and their friends, at the Sherman House, by Messrs. Gage Bros. and Walters.

SECTION A.

MATHEMATICS, PHYSICS, AND CHEMISTRY.

Chairman.

PROF. WM. CHAUVENET, OF ST. LOUIS.

Secretary.

PROF. GEO. F. BARKER, OF NEW HAVEN.

Sectional Committee.

PROF. T. H. SAFFORD, OF CHICAGO.
PROF. BENJ. SILLIMAN, OF NEW HAVEN.
PROF. E. N. HORSFORD, OF CAMBRIDGE.

————

TITLES OF PAPERS

For Monday, August 10th, 1868, in Section A.

1. On the Mathematical Investigations made for the Construction of the Illinois and St. Louis Bridge.
   By WILLIAM CHAUVENET. [20 minutes.]
2. On a Method of Measuring very Small Rectilinear Motions.
   By WILLIAM CHAUVENET. [10 m.]
3. On the Laws of Ocean Currents.
   By J. S. GRIMES. [30 m.]
4. Hough's Barometrograph as applied to the Investigation of the Storm Curve.   By J. H. COFFIN. [20 m.]
5. Remarks on the total Disturbance of the Barometrical Column.   By G. W. HOUGH. [15 m.]
6. The Profiles of Blast Furnaces.
   By THOMAS EGLESTON. [30 m.]
7. Fluorine a Constituent of the Brain
   By E. N. HORSFORD. [10 m.]

8. The Nature of Electric Discharge.
                    By O. N. Stoddard.   [14 m.]
9. On the Evaporative Power of the Sun near the Base of the Sierra Nevada, in Calaveras County, California.
                    By Benjamin Silliman.   [20 m.]
10. On the Relation between the Atomic Volume of Different Metals, and their Paramagnetic and Diamagnetic Properties.   By P. H. Vander Weyde.   [10 m.]
11. On the Molecular Arrangement of the Inorganic Acids.
                    By George F. Barker.   [30 m.]
12. Theory of the Prediction of Star Places.
                    By T. H. Safford.   [20 m.]
13. Remarks on the Secular Variations of the Eccentricities and Perihelia of the Eight Principal Planets.
                    By J. N. Stockwell.   [20 m.]
14. Description and Application of the Heliostat, and Method of Running True Meridian Lines in Surveying.
                    By Michael W. McDermott.   [20 m.]
15. Tides in Lakes.   By H. A. Newton.   [10 m.]

SECTION B.

GEOLOGY AND NATURAL HISTORY.

Chairman.

Prof. J. D. WHITNEY, of Cambridge, Mass.

Secretary.

Prof. E. D. COPE, of Philadelphia, Pa.

Sectional Committee.

A. H. WORTHEN, of Springfield, Ill.

Prof. O. C. MARSH, of New Haven, Conn.

Prof. THEO. GILL, of Washington, D. C.

TITLES OF PAPERS

For Monday, August 10th, 1868, at 2 P.M., in Section B.

1. Anatomical distinction of Vegetable Structure rectified, followed by the Circuit of Generation of Fresh Water Algæ.
   By T. C. Hilgard.
2. On Two New Fossil Trees, the oldest known, found by Rev. H. Herzer, in the Devonian Rocks of Ohio.
   By J. S. Newberry.
3. On *Elasmognathus* and its Relations to the Tapiridæ generally.   By Theodore Gill.
4. The Supposed Triassic Foot-marks in Kansas.
   By C. H. Hitchcock.
5. Sketch of the Topography, Geology and Antiquities of the Caucasus.   By F. Von Koschkull.
6. Fossil Fishes, Insects, Crustacea, etc., of the Coal Measures of Grundy County, Illinois.   By A. H. Worthen.
7. On the Preservation of Color in Fossils from Palæozoic Formations.   By O. C. Marsh.

PROGRAMME

TUESDAY, AUGUST 11*th*, 1868.

MORNING.

The General Session will be held in the Lecture Room of the First Baptist Church. The following Paper will be read:

On the Artistic Evidences of a Remote Colonization on the Great Western or American Continent, by Maritime People of Distinct Nationalities before the Modern Era.

By J. H. GIBBON.

EVENING.

Entertainment given to the members of the Association and their friends, by Messrs. GAGE BROS. and WALTERS, at the Sherman House.

STANDING COMMITTEE.

Dr. B. A. GOULD.	Prof. J. S. NEWBERRY.
Col. CHARLES WHITTLESEY.	Prof. WOLCOTT GIBBS.
Prof. JOSEPH LOVERING.	Prof. C. S. LYMAN.
Prof. SIMON NEWCOMB.	Dr. A. L. ELWYN.
Prof. H. L. EUSTIS.	Prof. H. A. NEWTON.
Prof. F. A. P. BARNARD.	Dr. C. C. PARRY.
Prof. S. D. TILLMAN.	Dr. J. H. RAUCH.

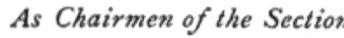

As Chairmen of the Sections:

SECTION A.	SECTION B.
Prof. WILLIAM CHAUVENET.	Prof. J. D. WHITNEY.

ADDITIONAL MEMBERS

Chosen to unite with Standing Committee as a Council for the Nomination of Officers.

SECTION A.	SECTION B.
Prof. ELIAS LOOMIS, of New Haven.	Prof. E. A. DALRYMPLE, of Baltimore.
Prof. CLEVELAND ABBE, of Cincinnati.	Prof. O. C. MARSH, of New Haven.
Prof. J. C. WATSON, of Ann Arbor.	Dr. C. A. WHITE, of Iowa City.
Prof. G. W. HOUGH, of Albany.	Col. J. W. FOSTER, of Chicago.

SUB-COMMITTEES OF THE STANDING COMMITTEE.

1. *Committee on Nominations:*

H. L. EUSTIS.	C. C. PARRY.

2. *Committee on Papers:*

J. S. NEWBERRY.	H. A. NEWTON.

3. *Committee on Hours and Business:*

J. H. RAUCH.	JOSEPH LOVERING.

NOTICES.

An entertainment will be given this evening to the Association, by Messrs. GAGE. BROS. and WALTERS, at the Sherman House. To this entertainment are invited, in addition to the Members of the Association, and their ladies and the friends entertaining them, the Members of the Academy of Sciences, the Historical Society, and the Astronomical Society, and the Faculties of the University and Medical Schools in Chicago and vicinity, the Officers of the Young Men's Association, the gentlemen of the Chicago Press, and the Officers of Railroad Companies centering in Chicago.

The new members, recently elected, are requested to come to the office of the Permanent Secretary and Treasurer, Parlor No. 3 Sherman House, to register their names, and pay their dues, if they have not already done so.

SECTION A.

MATHEMATICS, PHYSICS, AND CHEMISTRY.

Chairman.

PROF. WM. CHAUVENET, OF ST. LOUIS.

Secretary.

PROF. GEO. F. BARKER, OF NEW HAVEN.

Sectional Committee.

PROF. T. H. SAFFORD, OF CHICAGO.
PROF. BENJ. SILLIMAN, OF NEW HAVEN.
PROF. E. N. HORSFORD, OF CAMBRIDGE.

———

TITLES OF PAPERS

For Tuesday, August 11th, 1868, in Section A.

1. The Nature of Electric Discharge.
   By O. N. STODDARD. [14 m.]
2. On the Evaporative Power of the Sun near the Base of the Sierra Nevada, in Calaveras County, California.
   By BENJAMIN SILLIMAN. [20 m.]
3. On the Relation between the Atomic Volume of Different Metals, and their Paramagnetic and Diamagnetic Properties. By P. H. VANDER WEYDE. [10 m.]
4. On the Molecular Arrangement of the Inorganic Acids.
   By GEORGE F. BARKER. [30 m.]
5. Theory of the Prediction of Star Places.
   By T. H. SAFFORD. [20 m.]

6. Remarks on the Secular Variations of the Eccentricities and Perihelia of the Eight Principal Planets.
By J. N. Stockwell.

7. Description and Application of the Heliostat, and Method of Running True Meridian Lines in Surveying.
By Michael W. McDermott.

8. Tides in Lakes. By H. A. Newton.

9. On the Tides of Lake Michigan. By W. Ferrel.

10. Notes on the Defects of Lightning Rods.
By James Bushee.

11. Some New Facts and Views concerning Aluminum.
By Henry Wurtz.

12. The Application of Carbonic Acid Gas, in the Extinguishment of Fire. By E. L. Buttrick.

13. Atomic Motion. By H. F. Walling.

14. The Higher Law of Correlation. By O. N. Stoddard.

15. The Periodic Law in the Failure of Harvests and Inundations, with Suggestions as to their Insurance.
By George A. Leakin.

16. On Methods of Amalgamation in the Treatment of Gold Ores. By Benjamin Silliman.

17. On Redemption Periods of Monetary Values which involve Life Contingencies. By E. B. Elliott.

18. On the Metrical Unification of International Coinage.
By E. B. Elliott.

19. Exhibition of a New Selenograph. By Jerome Allen.

20. On a New Method of Measurement Map Drawing for Schools. By Jerome Allen.

21. Notes on the Origin of Bitumens, together with Experiments upon the Formation of Asphaltum. By S. F. Peckham.

22. Note on Epitrochoidal Teeth. By William Watson.

23. Remarks on the Galvanic Battery. By G. W. Hough.

24. On a Proposed New Mechanism for the Study of Galvanic Batteries. By G. W. Hough.

SECTION B.

GEOLOGY AND NATURAL HISTORY.

Chairman.

PROF. J. D. WHITNEY, OF CAMBRIDGE, MASS.

Secretary.

PROF. E. D. COPE, OF PHILADELPHIA, PA.

Sectional Committee.

A. H. WORTHEN, OF SPRINGFIELD, ILL.

PROF. O. C. MARSH, OF NEW HAVEN, CONN.

PROF. THEO. GILL, OF WASHINGTON, D. C.

———

TITLES OF PAPERS

For Tuesday, August 11th, 1868, *in Section B.*

MORNING.

1. On the Geology of the Mississippi Delta, and the Salt Deposit of Petite Anse.   By EUGENE W. HILGARD.
2. Fossil Fishes, Insects, Crustacea, etc., of the Coal Measures of Grundy County, Illinois.   By A. H. WORTHEN.
3. On the Preservation of Color in Fossils from Palæozoic Formations.   By O. C. MARSH.
4. Relations of the Metamorphoses of the Phosphates to Waste and Repair.   By E. N. HORSFORD.
5. On the Gradual Dessication of the Western Portions of North America.   By W. P. BLAKE.
6. The Yosemite Valley.   By J. D. WHITNEY.

EVENING.

7. On the Old Lake Beds of the Prairie Region.

By S. J. WALLACE.

8. Origin of the Prairies. By J. W. FOSTER.

9. On the Formation of Shells and Belemnites, and Phosphates of Iron at Mulica Hill, Gloucester County, N. J.

By A. B. ENGSTROM.

10. Superficial Geology of the Lake Shore near Chicago.

By J. S. JEWELL.

11. On Certain Physical Features of the Mississippi River.

By G. K. WARREN.

12. On the Surface Geology of the Basin of the Great Lakes and the Upper Mississippi Valley. By J. S. NEWBERRY.

13. Some Points in the Surface Geology of the Western Side of the American Continent. By J. D. WHITNEY.

14. On the Fuel Resources of Illinois. By A. H. WORTHEN.

15. On the Source of Muscular Power. By E. N. HORSFORD.

16. The Vertebral Type of the Cranium a Quinary one.

By T. C. HILGARD.

17. The Darwinian Theory of Development.

By CHARLES MORAN.

18. On the Geological Age and Equivalents of the Marshall Group. By A. WINCHELL.

150. **On the New Arctic Continent.** By W. W. WHEILDON.

151. On the Preservation of Meats. By JOHN GAMGEE.

ARRIVALS.

216. WILLIAM STIMPSON, Secretary of the Academy of Sciences, Chicago.

217. T. C. DUNCAN, Physician, Chicago — 265 W. Randolph Street.

218. E. L. BUTTRICK, Attorney, Chicago — Clifton House.

219. S. V. R. HICKCOX, Editor, Chicago — Richmond House.

220. EDWARD DANIELS, Geologist and Mining Engineer, Chicago — 287 Park Avenue.

221. G. K. WARREN, U. S. Army Corps of Engineers, New York.

222. E. B. ELLIOTT, U. S. Treasury, Washington, D. C.

223. W. C. HUNT, Physician and Microscopist, Chicago — 271 Erie Street.

224. ROBERT H. BROWNNE, Teacher, New York.

225. WALTER KATTE, Civil Engineer, Chicago — Sherman House.

226. BELDEN F. CULVER, Merchant, Chicago — Sherman House.

227. EDWIN M. HALE, Physician, Chicago — 65 Twenty-second Street.

228. HENRY M. STORRS, Clergyman, Brooklyn — Tremont House.

229. ALEXANDER REED, Clergyman, Philadelphia — Tremont House.

www.ingramcontent.com/pod-product-compliance
Lightning Source LLC
Chambersburg PA
CBHW030852260626
47169CB00008B/2510